The Purple Ponies

This book belongs to:

Princess _____

gigi, God's Little Princess™
series includes:

gigi, God's Little Princess™
(in book and DVD formats)
The Royal Tea Party*
The Perfect Christmas Gift
The Pink Ballerina*
The Purple Ponies
Gigi's Hugest Announcement DVD
(*indicates stories that appear on this DVD)

And just for boys:
will, God's Mighty Warrior™
series includes:

Will, God's Mighty Warrior™
The Mystery of Magillicuddy's Gold
The Creepy Caves Mystery

gigi

God's Little Princess™
The Purple Ponies

By Sheila Walsh
Illustrated by Meredith Johnson

THOMAS NELSON
Since 1798

NASHVILLE   DALLAS   MEXICO CITY   RIO DE JANEIRO   BEIJING

Published in Nashville, Tennessee, by Thomas Nelson. Thomas Nelson is a trademark of Thomas Nelson, Inc.

Thomas Nelson, Inc., books may be purchased in bulk for educational, business, fund-raising, or sales promotional use. For information, please e-mail SpecialMarkets@ThomasNelson.com.

Scripture quoted from *The Holy Bible, International Children's Bible*® (ICB). Copyright © 1986, 1988, 1999 by Thomas Nelson, Inc.

Library of Congress Cataloging-in-Publication Data

Walsh, Sheila, 1956–
  The Purple Ponies / Sheila Walsh ; illustrated by Meredith Johnson.
     p. cm. — (Gigi, God's little princess)
  Summary: When Gigi and her friend Frances try out for a soccer team, they learn that God gives people different gifts, and that each should use those gifts to shine.
  ISBN 978-1-4003-1124-8 (hardback)
 [1. Soccer—Fiction. 2. Christian life—Fiction. 3. Friendship—Fiction.] I. Johnson, Meredith, ill. II. Title.
PZ7.W16894Pur 2008
[E]—dc22
                                        2007018478

Printed in China
07 08 09 10 11 PHX 5 4 3 2 1

This book is
dedicated to all God's
princesses—the ones who
can kick the ball and the
ones who have a ball
cheering them on!

Gigi was not a boring princess.

She *did* like to dress up and was completely committed to pink, but she also loved trying new things! Today, Gigi turned her royal attention to soccer.

"Frances," Gigi said, attempting unsuccessfully to keep a soccer ball in the air, "today could change our lives forever!"

"Wow!" Frances replied with appropriate awe. "Forever is a *very* long time."

Gigi looked around. "It feels like it is taking forever to get through this line. There must be forty-two bazillion girls here!"

"Daddy, I am ready to get going. I am bursting with readiness. I have so much readiness it's coming out my ears!" Gigi said, bouncing up and down.

Gigi's daddy smiled. "Soccer is a very popular sport for princesses."

"But I am a natural athlete," Gigi replied.

"She's very good," Frances agreed. "Today she kicked her p.j.'s across the bedroom, and they landed right on Lord Fluffy's head."

"That is impressive!" Daddy agreed.

Finally, all the girls in front of them had signed in and received a nametag.

"Do you have any pink ones?" Gigi asked.

"We are the '*Purple* Ponies,'" the lady behind the sign-up desk replied. "We don't wear pink."

"That is tragic," Gigi whispered to Frances.

"Hello and welcome, girls. I'm Coach Prescott. Today, I will be picking fourteen girls to play with the Purple Ponies—seven for the first team and seven reserves. That means, unfortunately, that not everyone will be able to play on the soccer team this season."

"Poor things," Gigi whispered to Frances. "When we are chosen, we can look happy but not too happy. It wouldn't be nice for the poor girls who don't make the team."

"Girls," Coach Prescott began, "when I blow the whistle, take a ball and dribble it up to the line and back. Be in control of the ball at all times."

Gigi laughed so loudly that everyone turned to stare.

"Do you have something funny you would like to share with us all . . . Gigi?" Coach said, reading Gigi's nametag.

"No, ma'am," Gigi replied. "I do sincerely apologize for my not-so-royal behavior. It's . . . just that I've never been asked to drool on a ball before."

"That's not quite what I meant," Coach said with a smile. "Samantha Parker, will you please show all the new girls how to dribble a ball?"

"Oh . . . my . . . goodness!" Frances said to Gigi as they watched the team's star athlete control the ball.

"She is good," Gigi agreed. "I hope I don't make her feel bad when I show my stuff."

"Well, don't hold back, Gigi," Frances said.

"I couldn't, Frances," Gigi said with quiet dignity.
"It's just not in me."

Finally, it was their time to shine. The coach blew the whistle. Girls began to slowly dribble the ball toward the line.

But Gigi's first kick sent
her ball soaring across the field.

The next time, she accidentally
kicked it behind her.

On her third try, she tripped
and fell on top of the ball.

"My ball stinks!" Gigi said in frustration,
sprawled on the grass.

"It did seem a little . . . loose," Frances agreed.

"You were very good, Frances," Gigi said.

"Thank you, Gigi," Frances replied. "I had a friendly ball."

"Daddy, did you see my ball?" Gigi asked while they waited to see who would be on the team. "It was faulty. . . or it had a mouse inside it . . . or a magnet that was mysteriously being controlled from outer space," she suggested.

"Gigi," her daddy said, "it may be that soccer is just not for you."

Big tears began to roll down Gigi's cheeks.

"God has given you lots of gifts," her daddy explained. "It's your job to find out what those gifts are and use them to shine like God's princess."

"*Gigi! Look!*"

Frances shouted.

"Coach has posted the list."

Frances took off at breakneck speed as Gigi's daddy dried Gigi's eyes.

By the time Gigi reached Frances, she was heading back off the field.

"Well?" Gigi asked. "Are we Ponies? Are we Purple Ponies?"

"Not this time, Gigi," Frances said.

"Congratulations, Frances,"
Gigi's daddy said.

"Well, excuse me, Daddy," Gigi said.
"But you don't usually congratulate
someone for gross failuredom."

"What do you mean, Gigi?" Daddy said.
"Frances made it onto the team. Didn't
she tell you?"

Gigi stared at Frances. "I don't understand," she said.

"Gigi," Frances began, "when I saw my name and not your name on the list, I didn't know what to say. It wouldn't be as much fun without my very best friend."

"Well, Frances," Gigi said, "if God has made you good at soccer, you should use your gift. He might get cross if you're not out there shining!"

"But we wanted to be on the team together, Gigi," Frances said.

"I'm sure there's an answer to this problem, Frances," Gigi promised. "I just need to do some royal thinking about it."

First, they took Frances home. Then . . .

"Daddy, I've got it!" announced Gigi as Lord Fluffy and Tiara welcomed them home. "I've figured out how both Frances and I can be Purple Ponies. Listen to this:

Go, Ponies—Purple, Purple Ponies!
Kick the ball and show them all.
Go, Ponies, go!

"I'll be at Frances' games as a Purple Ponies cheerleader.
After all . . . I am very loud, so that must be one of my gifts!"

We all have different gifts.
Each gift came because of the
grace that God gave us.
Romans 12:6